It is not enough to prepare
our children for the world;
we also must prepare the world
for our children.

AMÉRICA
Is Her Name

by Luis J. Rodríguez

Illustrations by Carlos Vázquez

CURBSTONE PRESS

From the author:
This story is based on experiences I had working with Spanish-speaking children and their parents in the Pilsen barrio of Chicago on writing from their lives and imaginations. I want to thank the Chicago Teachers Center, which allowed me to consult for the public schools, particularly Anne Schultz and her team of poets, playwrights, and story tellers. I also want to thank the participants of the workshops, especially Mrs. Huízar and her four wonderful children who invited me into their home to reaffirm the poetry in all of us.

Text copyright © 1998 Luis J. Rodríguez
Illustrations copyright © 1998 Carlos Vázquez
Second printing: 1999

Curbstone Press is a 501(c)(3) nonprofit literary arts organization.
Publication of this book was made possible through support from the Andrew W. Mellon Foundation, the National Endowment for the Arts and the Connecticut Commission on the Arts. We are grateful for their support.

Printed in Hong Kong by Paramount Printing

Library of Congress Cataloging-in-Publication Data

Rodriguez, Luis J., 1954 -
    América is her name / by Luis J. Rodriguez. — 1st ed.
        p.   cm.
    Summary: A Mixteca Indian from Oaxaca, América Soliz, suffers from the poverty and hopelessness of her Chicago ghetto, made more endurable by a desire and determination to be a poet.
    ISBN 1-880684-40-3
    1. Mexican Americans — Juvenile fiction. [1. Mexican Americans — Fiction. 2. Poets — Fiction.] I. Title.
    PZ7.R61885Am   1996
    [Fic] — dc20   96-21345

CURBSTONE PRESS   321 Jackson Street   Willimantic, CT 06226
e-mail: books@curbstone.org   http://www.curbstone.org

A Mixteca Indian girl walks through the Pilsen barrio in Chicago. She has honey-brown skin and elongated eyes that are large and dark; her thick hair is in braids. . She was born in the mountains of Oaxaca. She still remembers the goats, pigs, and thatch-roofed house they once called home. Now she is in a strange place she can't even pronounce. She dreams of Oaxaca in Spanish.

América is her name. América Soliz. She is nine years old and has two brothers and a sister. Her mother's name is Nayeli, a Mixteco name which means "Flower of the Fields." América's father Oscar works the factories of southwest Chicago. He sleeps all day and works all night. She rarely sees him. Her uncle, Tío Filemón, lives with them. He also works. And he drinks. América dreams that he doesn't drink.

On her way to school América smiles at the man from Guerrero who sells "helados," real fruit ice cream sticks. She waves at the barber from Michoacán standing outside his shop waiting for customers. She sees teenagers standing around with nothing to do. She smiles at them. They smile back and continue talking.

Rounding the next corner, she sees a boy walking down the street. Some guys call out to him. He spins around, pulls a gun out of his waist band, and shoots at the group. The others run, but América just stands there. Nobody is hit. She stares at the young man, who then turns toward her. His face is a scowl; his eyes cold and dark. He puts the gun back into his waist band, and walks away.

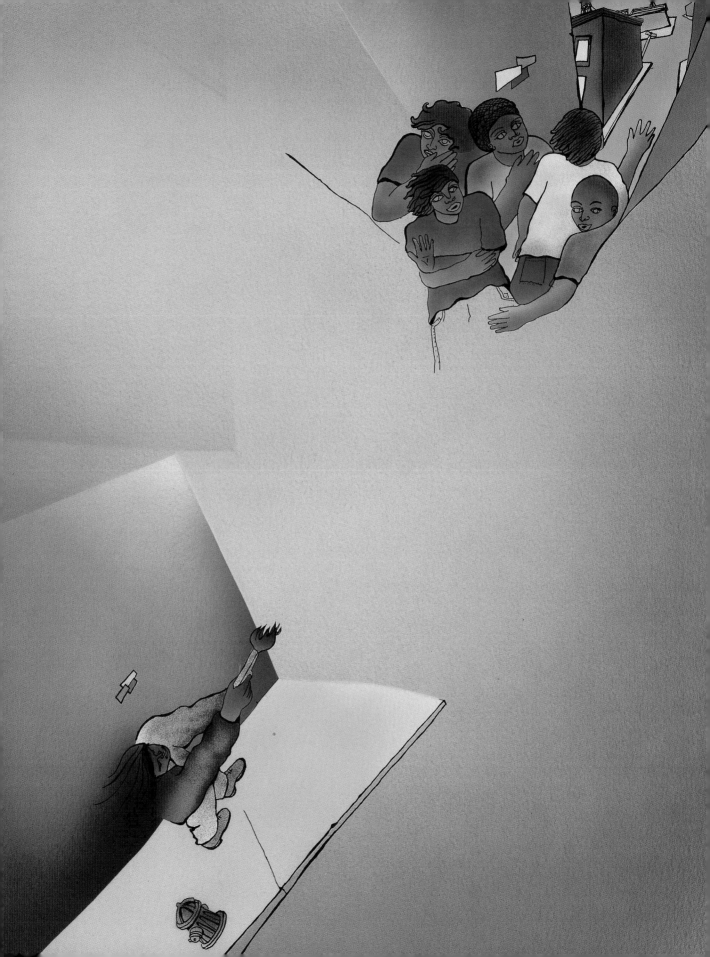

When América reaches her English as a Second Language class, she slips quietly into the room as Miss Gable is yelling at the students. "Sit down! Be quiet!"

América sits at the back of the room and says nothing. América used to talk all the time. In her village, she greeted the animals in Spanish mixed with a few Mixteco words. She sang to the morning. She recited the many poems taught her since she was a baby. She had a voice—strong, open and free. Somehow, in Chicago, she has lost this voice. She thinks hard about her faraway home that is beginning to fade from her memory.

Yesterday as she passed Miss Gable and Miss Williams in the hallway, she heard Miss Gable whisper, "She's an illegal." How can that be—how can anyone be illegal! She is Mixteco, an ancient tribe that was here before the Spanish, before the blue-eyed, even before this government that now calls her "illegal." How can a girl called América not belong in America?

But today something in school is different. Miss Gable introduces Mr. Aponte, a Puerto Rican poet who is visiting. Miss Gable tells him they are a "difficult" class. Mr. Aponte looks at everyone and then asks in Spanish, "Who likes poetry?" Many hands dart up. "Who wants to recite some poetry?" he asks. América quickly raises her hand high. Mr. Aponte asks her to stand and recite a poem. América closes her eyes and rocks with the rhythms of the Spanish words she recites. When she finishes, the class explodes in applause. Mr. Aponte is pleased. Miss Gable just frowns.

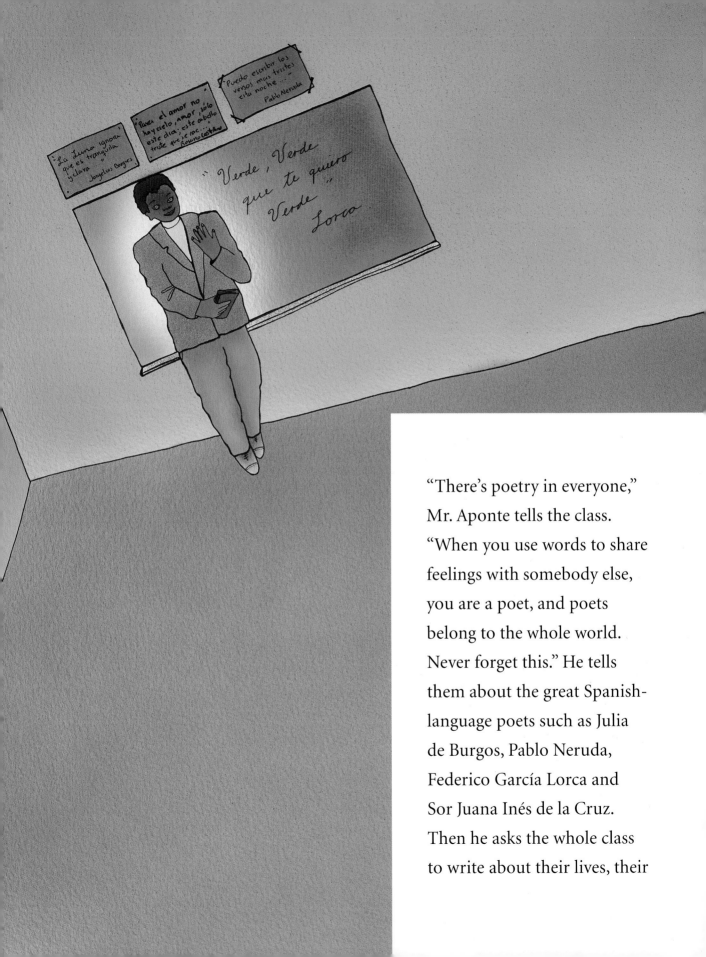

"There's poetry in everyone," Mr. Aponte tells the class. "When you use words to share feelings with somebody else, you are a poet, and poets belong to the whole world. Never forget this." He tells them about the great Spanish-language poets such as Julia de Burgos, Pablo Neruda, Federico García Lorca and Sor Juana Inés de la Cruz. Then he asks the whole class to write about their lives, their

memories, and their feelings. Some of the children can't write very well. Mr. Aponte says this is okay. "Don't worry about spelling or grammar—that will come later. Write in Spanish or English, whichever feels comfortable." América starts writing. She has so much to write about, she thinks she won't be able to stop.

When América gets home, she hears her dad yelling. He has been laid off from the factory. The family gathers for supper around a wooden table in the small kitchen. Her mother tells her father angrily: "I was called a 'wetback' at the market today. No matter what we do —we don't belong." Tío Filemón comes in the room, drunk and loud. "Never say you don't belong," he says. "We belong anywhere, everywhere. Once you believe you don't belong, you'll be homeless forever. Maybe we'll go back to Oaxaca, maybe we won't. For now, this is home."

After supper, as América sits at the kitchen table to write, her dad walks by.
"What are you doing, m'ija?" he asks.
"I'm writing," she says.
"Writing? Is this for school?"
"No, papi, it's for me—I'm writing a poem for me."
"Don't waste your time. Where are you going to go with writing? Learn to clean house, to take care of your brothers and sisters. Writing for yourself won't pay the bills."

América is sad. "Will this be my life?" she wonders. "Not to write. To clean houses, get married, have children. To wait for the factory to feed us." She sees in her mind all of the sullen faces that look out of third-floor windows when she walks to school and the desperate men without jobs standing on street corners. They all seem trapped, like flowers in a vase, full of song and color, yet stuck in a gray world where they can't find a way out. "Will this be my life?"

Mr. Aponte stopped coming to América's class; he was only there as part of a special program. Miss Gable is yelling at everyone for talking out of turn, for not doing their work right. América wishes Mr. Aponte was back. She writes her stories and poems secretly now because there's no one to read them to.

At home everyone is worried. There are days when the family doesn't have enough money for food. Tío Filemón works, but mainly to help with the rent and buy beer. Her father paces the rooms and hallways, always angry.

América is quiet and sad. Nayeli sits down at the table with América and says, "M'ija write something for me." América gives her a pencil and a piece of paper and says, "Mama, you write something, too."

Every day after school, Nayeli and América sit around the table and write. Nayeli writes about long-gone days in the rancho, about the tall grasses and burly oxen. About her many cousins and other family who always visited. América smiles as her mother struggles with the words. They share their stories with each other. Soon América's older brother is taking part, and even the little ones join in.

Tío Filemón reads one of América's
stories and tells her it is very good. Her dad
comes in and says, "You're still writing? What did I
tell you about this!"

Tío Filemón looks at him hard and says, "Yes, she is very
good. You got quite a daughter here."

"Oh what do you know—you can't even write,"
América's father responds.

"Yes, that's true. All I can do is work with my hands and
gulp a few beers," Tío Filemón says. "But your daughter
is going to do more than you or me. I can see it. She will
bloom, long after we've rotted on the vine."

A few days later América burst into the kitchen. "Mama, mama, tengo un cien!" she says. "I got a hundred on my writing assignment. Even Miss Gable liked it." Nayeli beams proudly. "I knew you could do it! You are a poet." Her dad looks up from the television and says, "Well, what do you know. Maybe I've got a poet for a daughter." He stands up. América thinks he is going to yell at her. Instead, he hugs her real tight. "M'ija," he says. "Don't worry, I'll find a job again. I'll work hard, every day, every night if I have to. It's good you're writing poetry." América smiles. Tío Filemón winks at her and says "You'll be a real poet."

A real poet. That sounds good to the Mixteca girl, who some people say doesn't belong here. A poet, América knows, belongs everywhere.